My Three Orc Dads

My Three Orc Dads

BY DOMINIC N. ASHEN

4 Horsemen
Publications, Inc.

4 Horsemen Publications, Inc.
1497 Main St. Suite 169
Dunedin, FL 34698
4horsemenpublications.com
info@4horsemenpublications.com

Cover by Oxford
Typesetting by Autumn Skye
Editor Tilda M. Cooke

Library of Congress Control Number: 2021948920

Audio ISBN: 978-1-64450-422-2
Ebook ISBN: 978-1-64450-423-9
Print ISBN: 978-1-64450-424-6

Table of Contents

$J + K + O + D =$ 

Chapter 1

"I still don't understand why I can't just stay home by myself."

"Because I still cannot trust you to stay out of trouble while I am gone."

It's the late in the morning, and the two of us are walking through the streets of V'rok'sh Tah'lj. We're headed to see Khazak's parents, who I will be spending the next few days with. Without Khazak.

"I don't need a babysitter!" Though the whining might say differently.

"They are not babysitting you," Khazak tries to reassure me.

I know he's right, but the worst part about it is it doesn't even really feel like babysitting—it feels like *pet*sitting.

"Also, as I told you, this is a *diplomatic* mission," he points out as we approach his parents' home. "We are meeting with the delegations of four different cities, and you do not even speak the language. Any of them."

"I'm learning!" I roll my eyes at his answer as he knocks on the door.

"There you are." Rurig, Khazak's father, answers the door with one of his husbands, Jarek, right behind him. Between the two, Rurig is a few years older, a little shorter, and a lot wider, with a generous belly that I have seen shaking on more than one occasion when the man laughs. Jarek, who is maybe ten years his husband's younger, sports a neatly trimmed mustache and goatee that matches the short black hair on his head, as opposed to the longer brown on his husband.

"Sorry for the delay, Ruda," Khazak apologizes as we walk inside—we were supposed to be here twenty minutes ago, but I might have dragged things out so I could try and change his mind. Obviously, it didn't work. "We needed to make sure he had everything for his stay. Thank you again for watching him."

"You know we will take good care of him, son." Rurig reaches out to ruffle my hair affectionately as I'm passed over to them.

"Where is Orda?" Khazak asks about the location of his *third* father, Orlun.

"Your aunts needed help moving some furniture and he volunteered. He will be back by dinner," Rurig assures him.

"Give him my love." Khazak hugs his fathers before hugging me. "Please behave yourself."

"I always behave," I grumble as I hug him back. "... Come back soon, 'kay?"

"See you in a few days, puppy." With a final kiss to my forehead, he's gone, and the front door closes.

"I hope you are hungry because it is almost lunch-time!" Rurig announces happily, rubbing his hands together. Is he ever not cooking?

"Uh, yes sir. That sounds good." Without Khazak here, I'm feeling a little off-balance.

"Heh, 'sir?' I like you, kid." He ruffles my hair again and turns to Jarek. "Will you take him to Khazak's old room to get settled while I get started on lunch?"

"Follow me, David." Jarek puts his hand on my shoulder as he leads me away.

"Thank you." I follow him into the living room and then down a hall. I've only been here once before so I don't *exactly* know where I'm going.

"Here we are." Jarek opens the door to reveal a familiar looking room before stepping inside.

It's as threadbare as I remember it: a bed, a few bookcases, and a desk in one corner. There's a couple of old looking bows hanging from the walls, but that's it. Cozy, if not a little boring. I set my bag on the bed, wondering if I should bother unpacking. All I brought was a few changes of clothes and a couple of Khazak's books. And maybe something else for late at night.

"We changed the sheets before you got here," Jarek informs me. "You know, I do not think anyone has slept in this room in over ten years."

"Not since Khazak moved out?" I think the timeline matches up, at least.

"Yes." Jarek nods his head. "Just a few years after they finished their schooling, Khazak and Ragnar rented a too-small apartment together for a few years while he saved up to buy his current home. I made a lot of his furniture myself, actually."

"It all looks really nice." Khazak once pointed out where Jarek worked to me, a half-tree nursery, half-carpentry business. "What's it like not having them in the house anymore?"

"It always gets quieter around here when one of the children moves out, but I suppose it will be much stranger in a few years after Ursza and Ignatz are finally gone. Those two are staying with friends for the next few days." He considers my question for a moment. "You know, I cannot say I ever saw myself one day being the father to five children. Especially seeing as three of them were here before I was."

"Is it weird being a step-father?" It's not something I've ever considered myself.

"Perhaps a little at first, but that was largely due to how Orlun and Rurig introduced them to me." I knew Khazak did not like Jarek when he first came around, but I haven't heard this story. "I was probably right around your age when I met the two of them. It was a rather...*hectic* time for the city. They were already married, and I assumed I was just in for a bit of fun with them, but we kept on seeing each other. Then one day, Rurig was injured and Orlun asked me to watch their three children. Children I did not even know existed at that point."

"Oh, wow." Three kids is a lot to dump on someone by surprise.

"That was my feeling as well," he grumbles slightly. "I was *not* happy to suddenly be responsible for child-care, but I was willing to do it for them. It all worked out in the end."

"I heard Khazak wasn't exactly your biggest fan." Ayla said he *hated* him, but that seems harsh.

Jarek chuckles at my comment. "He was young, and he had his reasons. I am very proud to be able to call myself his father today."

"Well, you guys raised a great son," I compliment with a smile. "Very responsible, if not a little heavy handed."

"He gets that from his father," he muses.

"Which one?" I ask.

Jarek laughs at my stupid joke. "Let us get you unpacked and fed."

"Oh no, that's okay." I try to stop Jarek from reaching for my bag on the bed. "I can take care of that—"

I'm too late, and he empties the contents of my bag onto the bed. Out come my clothes, the books, my toothbrush...and the wooden plug, bottle of oil, and charm I use to keep myself clean and open when I'm playing with my butt. My face, no, my whole body turns red. What?! Three days is a long time, okay? I've become accustomed to a certain amount of sex.

"Well, I see my son has certainly been training you properly." He eyes the large-ish plug on the bed. It's *barely* thicker than Khazak's cock. Not that Jarek would know that.

"I am *so* sorry," I scramble to try and cover the toy with my clothes. "You weren't supposed to—"

"Nothing to be ashamed of, *pup*." Jarek uses the nickname Khazak gave me, then pulls the shirt off of the plug and picks it up. "Rather impressive if you are already able to take something this large."

"I, uh, I'm..." I have no idea how to take that compliment.

"Something the matter, David?" Jarek steps closer, still holding the plug.

What is going on right now? What is he—*aaannnd* he's kissing me. He's good too, and it takes me a solid five seconds for the full implication of this to hit me. Then I pull back in shock.

"What are you... We can't..." I am almost positive that kissing my owner's stepdad is *not* something I should be doing. "I'm sorry!"

"Did Khazak not tell you?" Jarek searches my face in concern.

"Tell me what?" This seems like a pretty big thing to neglect mentioning.

"That it is tradition for an *avakesh* to spend a night with his *kavan's* parents." My eyes go wide at Jarek's revelation.

"No... He... He did not say anything like that." *Is he serious?*

"We understand if this makes you uncomfortable," Jarek tells me, moving his hands behind his back and hiding the plug from view. "There would be no offense taken if you preferred not to act on this tradition, but I assure you, there is absolutely nothing wrong with it in our culture."

I take a moment to look at Jarek, a lot more closely than I have before. He's not a bad looking guy. He has a slimmer build than Khazak, but he's still bigger than me, though his height is actually right around mine. His neatly trimmed goatee frames his short white tusks perfectly, and there's something about the worry in his eyes that makes him look sweet. If I'm being perfectly honest, there's also a part of me that just really, really wants Khazak's parents to like me. Shit, am I gonna do this? I mean, it is a tradition, right? "...Are you sure this is okay?"

"Of course, pup." He steps closer, tossing the plug on the bed as he does. "Now how about you just relax and let me take over, so you can stop worrying so much."

"...Okay, sir." I nod, my mouth suddenly feeling dry.

"You *are* going to be fun," Jarek tells me before kissing me again.

Yeah, he's good at this. Maybe as good as Khazak, but I don't have a lot of male-based kisses to compare to. One of his hands comes up to cup my face while the other snakes around my waist to the small of my back, pulling us closer together. I allow myself to be touched and manipulated but otherwise just stand there, too nervous to know what to do with my own hands or *anything* beyond kissing back.

Sensing my hesitation, Jarek breaks our kiss and begins unbuttoning his shirt, pulling it off with a small smirk. Then his hands reach for the buttons of my own, chuckling when my fingers fumble when I try to help. Once he gets my shirt off, he maneuvers us onto the bed on our sides, and we resume kissing.

From the way we are laying, I can feel Jarek's erection pressing into my thigh, my own dick doing the same. Can't say I'm not enjoying this, even if it does seem weird as hell. Jarek's hands begin to slide up and down my sides, back and chest, stopping to tease the spots where I seem the most sensitive. Finally feeling a little bold, I try to copy him, though I have less luck at finding those sensitive areas than he does.

Eventually, I feel him brushing up against the front of my pants, and then his hands are reaching for my buttons again. I have to fight against the urge to stop him, though it's significantly easier than the last time. He does the same to himself, saving me from making an awkward attempt.

I gasp into his mouth as he palms my dick through the pouch of my jockstrap. Pulling the fabric to the side, he frees my cock from its confines, grasping it firmly in his hand. He lowers the waistband of his underwear, freeing himself and pushing forward to rub our lengths together. He places them side by side, holding them together in one hand. He's a little larger than I am, both in length and thickness, but he looks to be a *lot* more manageable than Khazak.

"Not bad, boy," Jarek tells me as he strokes our cocks together. "But how do you taste?"

Faster than I am expecting, Jarek flips his body so that his head is near the foot of the bed. Well, it's really closer to my dick. As is his to mine, the green appendage twitching slightly in front of my face. I just manage to work up the nerve to reach for it when the warm heat of his mouth envelops me. *Oh fuck.* I hump forward slightly, wanting more of the wet heat on my cock.

He doesn't stop me from moving my hips, but he does use a hand to reach for my head and pull it toward his own crotch. Happy to prove I can take direction, I open my mouth to swallow him down. Jarek moans around my dick, the vibrations providing some added sensation to his sucking. Grabbing the base with my hand, I start to mimic his movements, moving my mouth up and down his length while holding him steady.

We're lost in the haze of this double blowjob for some time. I *think* this position is called a sixty-nine? I'll have to ask. Not now though. Now it's just me, Jarek, the heat of his mouth, the solid way his dick feels against my tongue, the taste of his pre-cum... When I feel him start trying to hump forward, I actually think I might be getting him close, but then he pulls out of my mouth completely.

"I do not want to cum yet," he explains, pulling off my cock for a moment. "You, however... I told you I wanted to *taste* you."

He swallows me right back down, his head rapidly bobbing up and down the top half of my cock. He covers the other half with his hand, stroking me in time with his mouth using his spit to slick the way. Without anything to occupy my mouth, I moan aloud, arms reaching out to hold onto Jarek's leg to keep steady.

"I'm... I'm getting close," I warn, but he only doubles his efforts in response, which I take as permission to let go.

I bite my lip as I cum, wanting to hold back the noise. It still feels like we're doing something very wrong, which of course makes cumming so much more intense. Each shot fills his mouth, and he's no longer sucking or stroking, just swallowing. When I'm finished, he pulls off, smacking his lips with a grin.

"Not bad," he says as he slides off the mattress to stand, bending over to kiss me as I recover, wanting me to taste for myself. "My turn now."

Still standing, he "helps" me to flip so that I am laying half on my stomach, half on my right side. He has me hike my left leg up and bends it, like I'd be kneeing someone in the stomach if I were standing. Keeping my right leg straight, he climbs onto the bed behind me and straddles it. Oh fuck, already? I don't complain or ask for a break though, too desperate to please my owner's fathers.

After searching the pile of my things for the charm, he reaches under me to place it against my stomach, tossing it to the side once it's finished. I hear the cork on the vial of oil open, and then a pair of slick fingers are prodding my ass. I gasp when they come into contact with my hole, gently but firmly pressing inside.

"Very nice," Jarek comments, using the hand not inside of me to squeeze my rump.

Thanks to all the "practice" I've been getting with Khazak, prepping me doesn't take long, and soon something that feels distinctly cock-shaped is slipping between my cheeks. His other hand is still on my ass, spreading me open as he guides himself to his target. Feeling the slick head pressing against me, I brace myself for what comes next. I've never been fucked after cumming like that, and I'm a little nervous about how sensitive I might be.

I groan when he finally breaches me, sliding forward slowly until I feel his pubic hair scratching against me. I was right, I am more sensitive, the fullness joined by the feeling of something that isn't quite pleasure and isn't quite pain. Fully seated, he settles more of his weight on my leg, relaxing into the position. I try to do the same, but it's a little difficult with a dick inside of you. At least he's not as big as his stepson, which isn't a sentence anyone should ever think. *Oh gods, what am I doing?*

"So tight," Jarek mutters from above me.

He grabs me with both hands now, half by the ass and half by the hip from this angle. He presses himself forward while pulling me back, squeezing us together and making me moan. I grab the pillow in front of me to muffle my noise, just in time for him to pull back a few inches and thrust back in. The pain-pleasure feeling grows more intense when he starts to fuck me in earnest, steadily sliding himself forward and back as he straddles my thigh.

It doesn't take long for Jarek to get comfortable with his movements, and he starts picking up speed, his grip growing even stronger. He changes his angle of attack, using his hands on my ass to lift himself up when he pulls back, and letting him slide back in at an angle that feels like he's going even deeper. This also has the effect of pressing me deeper into the mattress, pushing me to lie more on my stomach. I groan, squeezing the pillow as the familiar sensation of a prostate orgasm starts to build. *How do they always do that?*

"Relax. Let it happen, boy." Jarek ends his instruction with a small spank to my ass.

"It's not...that...easy," I growl out, still not quite there.

That seems to spur Jarek on, and a second later, his thrusts get even stronger and faster. I barely have time to prepare myself when I finally feel the dam break, my toes curling as the orgasm washes over me. From my position, my chest flat against the bed with most of Jarek's weight pinning my lower half down, I can't do much else but take it.

"Good boy, that is what I wanted." He leans forward to stroke a hand down my sweaty back. "Now, I believe I said it was my turn."

Apparently having gotten what he was after, Jarek continues these tactics, his grip on my ass still solid. The steady sound of slapping fills the room as his crotch slams into my ass over and over, both of us sweating. I cry out into the pillow when I feel another orgasm starting to build. I have no idea how close he is, but I'm not sure how much more of this I can take.

"Almost...there..." he grits out above me. *Oh thank god.*

After just a few more thrusts, Jarek slams his hips down without pulling back, at least not until he's done unloading this first spurt of cum. He pulls back, doing the same with every subsequent shot, until he's finished, panting above me, still straddling my leg. I feel sweat drip down onto my back when he leans forward, using his hands to hold himself up while he catches his breath. The pressure of the orgasm begins to fade, and I whimper when I feel Jarek slip out of me as he lays down behind me in the bed.

"We can rest for a little bit..." Jarek mumbles against my neck, my eyes already closed before he even finishes talking.

"What the hell is going on in here?" My eyes shoot back open when I hear Rurig's voice. *Oh gods. How do I explain this?*

Chapter 2

I'm frozen in place at Rurig's sudden entrance, his question hanging in the air. I'm laying naked in his son's old bed, with his equally naked husband behind me, spooning me with his arm thrown over my waist. Why he isn't answering I don't know, but it's not like I have any idea what to say! I'm facing a wall, but my eyes are still squeezed tight, trying to will myself invisible. *I can't believe I did this, I shouldn't be here, I have to—*

"I told you to help him get settled, not fuck him," Rurig scoffs, sounding more annoyed than any-thing else.

Jarek groans as he rolls onto his back, away from me. "You are just jealous because I got to him first." *Wait, what?*

"No, I am *unhappy* because there is a *tree* sitting in my backyard that you promised to turn into firewood this morning." I dare to roll over myself, opening one eye to see Rurig standing in the doorway, hand on his hip, giving Jarek a very unimpressed look.

"Not a tree, just a log." I can hear Jarek roll his eyes as he slides off the bed, bending over to reach for his pants, "but I will take care of that right away, dear." With a kiss to his husband's cheek, he throws his pants over his shoulder and exits the room.

"You did not even wait until he was unpacked," Rurig calls down the hall after him, before turning to me. "Sorry about that. Go ahead and finish, then get cleaned up and come find me in the kitchen."

"Uh, sure. Yes sir." I nod at the smiling orc, as if I'm not laying here naked with his husband's cum leaking out of my... *Get your shit together, David.* "I'll be right there."

I flop back onto the bed when he leaves, covering my face with my hands and resisting the urge to scream. What the hell did Khazak sign me up for? Once I'm composed, I roll off the bed, grabbing my clothes from the floor. After redressing, I fold and pile the rest of my things on Khazak's old desk. Time to get cleaned up.

I peek my head out of the door, for some reason feeling shy that someone might see me heading to the bathroom to clean up after...*that.* I quietly make my way down the hall, washing my hands and face in the sink before grabbing some toilet paper and making sure I'm not leaving any wet spots on the inside of my pants... These last few weeks have been weird.

Once I'm feeling presentable, I head for the kitchen. I'm actually a little impressed that I can remember where everything is, considering I've only been here a handful of times. Still, I pause just outside the doorway, my nervousness creeping back up. I know Jarek said everything we did was fine, and Rurig seemed almost *bored* by what he saw, but it still feels like I'm doing something wrong.

"That you out there, David?" *Damn orc hearing.*

"Yeah, sorry. Right here." I try to enter without looking too sheepish.

The kitchen is a lot less busy than it was the last time I was in here. Less warm too, probably because there aren't twenty different things being cooked. Rurig is leaning against the counter when I enter, a knife in his hand and a decent sized slab of meat behind him. There's still no sign that he's shocked at catching me in bed with one of his husbands, just a smile.

"You any good with a knife?" he asks, holding up the one in his hand.

"Depends. Do you mean in the kitchen or a fight?" *There's that nervous joke-making habit.*

"Well seeing as we are *in* a kitchen," he gestures to the room with his free hand, "I obviously meant a fight. Yours is over there. Defend yourself!" The chubby, one-legged orc holds out his knife hand threateningly as he slides into a fighting stance.

I fail to hold in the snort of laughter, happy that my joke was at least well-received.

"What? Think you can take me?" he asks with a twinkle in his eye before standing up straight. "Seriously though, *are* you any good with a knife in the kitchen?"

"Pretty decent." *In both cases, actually.* "What do you need me to do?"

"I set you up over here." He points to a spot to his left where a cutting board sits. "I need you to peel and then cut those into cubes about this big." He holds up his finger and thumb as an example. "Then toss them in that pot." He points to a large pot sitting on the stove, steam slowly wafting out of the top.

"Yes sir." That's the second time I've called him sir. Thanks, years of training.

I step up to my station, a wooden cutting board with a knife on top, and some already-peeled vegetables on the counter behind it. I see carrots, potatoes, and those orange-colored potatoes Khazak told me are named camotes, but that most people who speak Common just call sweet potatoes.

"Picked those up just for you," Rurig says on my right. Orc diets are mostly meat-based. "Have you done much cooking?"

"When I was growing up, I spent a lot of time in the kitchen with my mom." I pick up my knife and grab a potato to start cutting. "I have three siblings, so she was pretty much always cooking. Everyone helped out, but I probably spent more time in there with her than anyone else. Definitely more than my brothers. All of us would be talking while mom told us what to do. I just thought it was fun."

"Seems like you enjoyed taking orders from a young age." I look over to catch Rurig's toothy grin. "Cooking is important for any family, especially large ones. You would be surprised at the things you pick up when you spend most of your time over a stove. Tell me, when you would fight with your siblings, did your mother ever make the two of you help her at the same time?"

"Yeah. A lot, actually." *And it annoyed the crap outta me.*

"And by the time you were finished cooking, were you still fighting?" Rurig asks next while I grab another potato.

"No, not usually." *Huh.* I walk the cutting board over to the pot and drop in the potato cubes. "I've never really thought about that before."

"A trick I have used myself many times." The larger orc chuckles. "Your mother sounds like a smart woman."

"Yeah, she's pretty great." I grab a carrot with a smile. "When I was little, I would ask to help her anytime I could, but once I got older, I started to worry about being called a uh, 'momma's boy,' so I stopped. She never stopped asking me though, even after all the times I'd tell her no or find some excuse to get out of it. It wasn't until I was even older that I realized that cooking together like that was her way of spending time with us. So, I started helping her again, as much as I could before I left for the knight academy."

"I learned most of what I know from my mother. I was an only child, but as you can see, she still did a lot of cooking." The orc rubs his generous belly, moving his now-sliced meat over to a pan on the stove. "There was no one else to help, so she passed on all her skills, recipes, everything she could, to me. She passed three years ago. I still have the recipe book she wrote for me when I married Orlun, though I probably know everything in there by heart."

"Is it a big book?" Not that it sounds any less impressive.

"Over ninety different dishes." *Holy crap.* "Do you remember any of your own mother's recipes?" he then asks, meat hitting the pan with a sizzle.

"Not really. I was never great at remembering that stuff." *Anything involving numbers or measurements, really.* "I can think of how to make a few basic things, like cookies, but the more complicated stuff would take a lot of guessing. She wrote some of them down for me before I left, but there was a lot less freedom in the kitchens at the academy. I still liked working kitchen duty more than the other work assignments, but it's not like I got to pick what we made. Plus, I don't think my mom's recipes would have been very useful in feeding a fort full of soldiers."

"That is true. The more mouths you have to feed, the more creative you must get," he tells me as I add more vegetables to the pot.

Whatever it is, it's starting to smell good. I look in the top, seeing my cut vegetables mixing with the other ingredients, mostly spices and some greens. The broth is thicker, almost gravy-like, so obviously we are making some kind of stew; venison from the smell of it, which seems to be the meat of choice around here. Rurig starts to add the slices of venison to the pot as soon as they are done cooking, fat still dripping off.

"Alright. Nothing to do now except wait for this to finish," Rurig declares, putting a lid on the pot once we're both done adding things. "Got a few hours to kill. Come with me. We need to get you cleaned up again."

Rurig leads me to their bedroom instead of the bathroom like I'm expecting. When I see the extra-large bed—that is shared nightly by no less than *three* men—I feel a twinge of anxiety, but when I enter the attached bathroom, I understand why he brought me here instead: it's *huge*. Twice as big as the other one and at least three times the size of Khazak's. Against one wall is a stone counter with two sinks, a wide mirror hanging on the wall just above it. Instead of a tub, the other wall houses a large shower big enough for at least two people, maybe more. It's almost like the group showers we had at the academy, but this one has walls that reach the ceiling made of what looks like colored glass that's been melded together.

Rurig heads to the far sink, turning the water on before pulling off his shirt. He's got some blood on him, not his own thankfully. Cutting meat is just a lot messier than chopping vegetables. He's not a bad looking man with his longer hair and dark brown beard. He's got a generous chest and stomach, both of his nipples pierced with gold rings.

Below the waist, he's got a butt to match his belly, and I suddenly understand Khazak's obsession with spanking. I wonder if he got that from his other dad? Further down, his left leg has been amputated below the knee—an old injury from his time in the city's militia. In its place is a prosthetic made of wood and metal, extending straight downward maybe a third of a meter before the end curves into a "C" shape. It almost looks like the handle of a walking cane, but flipped upside down. I've never noticed it giving him any trouble, but he's had decades to master it.

Realizing that I'm staring, I grab the closer sink, lathering up and rinsing my hands. As I finish, I feel Rurig squeeze out of the room behind me, his stomach brushing against my back. When I'm done drying off and exit, I'm surprised to see him sitting on the edge of the bed waiting for me, still shirtless.

"Alright. Get over here so I can see what we are working with." The orc crooks a finger at me.

"Huh? Woah!" I only take a single step toward him before he grabs my shirt to pull me closer, both hands working to undo my belt and yank down my pants in record time.

"Not bad," he comments after sticking his hand in the pouch of my jockstrap, grabbing my cock.

"Uhhhh..." I'm frozen in place, unsure of how to proceed with the man's hand on my dick.

"I figured Jarek explained all of this already." He raises an eyebrow at me, still holding on to my now-growing dick. What? That's what happens when it's grabbed! "Or did he leave you too drained for more?"

"Sorry. He did explain it." I nod. "I just was—"

"Good." He stands, turning us both around and pushing me to sit on the bed with way more grace than I would have expected for someone his size. "Now finish taking your clothes off."

I look up at the half-naked orc, already undoing the belt around his own waist and pull my shirt off with a sigh. I mean, I already fucked one of Khazak's dads, right? Before I can reach for my underwear, Rurig kneels down and hooks his fingers in my waistband, sliding them down and off my feet. With both hands on my thighs, he spreads my legs and shuffles forward, eyeing my crotch like it's a piece of candy.

After grabbing and giving me an appreciative stroke, he leans forward and wordlessly takes me into his mouth. I grab at the sheets under me as I feel the heat wrap around me, making my cock pulse. He slowly continues his journey downward until I can feel his nose against my groin, his tongue stroking against the base of my shaft. *Fuck*, he's good at that.

Finally pulling back a minute later, he starts to slowly bob up and down, coaxing my dick to full hardness with his lips and tongue. He hums to himself happily when he feels me grow to my full size in his mouth, pulling off with a wet pop. He reaches one hand up to hold me steady as he eyes my cock once more.

"Nope, not bad at all." He strokes his hand up and down my spit-slick shaft. "Pretty tasty too."

I moan as he dives back into my crotch, a hungry twinkle in his eyes. There's no more teasing. He's suddenly a man on a mission, and that mission is to suck my dick. I keep my hands fisted in the sheets, too timid to reach down and grab his head. My hips don't seem to get the same message though, happily humping up into the man's warm mouth each time he moves down, the blunt face of his tusks bumping lightly against me.

Eventually, Rurig has enough and stands after pulling off me again, the cool air making my spit-covered dick twitch. I watch him silently walk over to a nightstand, his butt and belly bouncing slightly with each step. He opens the drawer, retrieving a vial of *something*, probably oil.

"Go ahead and move farther up the bed, pup." He uncorks the vial as he speaks, dribbling some out into his hand. "Flat on your back."

"Uh, yes sir." I nod and slide back, turning myself so that I'm in the requested position.

Rurig climbs onto the bed and shuffles forward on his knees, careful not to let his prosthetic catch on any of the sheets I've messed up. He pulls my legs together and straddles me, looking down like I'm his favorite meal as reaches behind to prepare himself with oil-covered fingers. Satisfied with his handiwork, he reaches forward with the same oil-slick hand to grab my cock, spreading whatever is left over as he strokes me.

Rurig moves farther up until his thighs are above my waist, the bottom of my dick rubbing against his balls and taint. His own cock is hard and heavy, hanging over my belly and under his. It's thick, much thicker than mine, but not quite as long, though I guess that could just be because of said belly. Gripping himself with his slick hand, he pushes down on my chest as he grinds himself onto my cock with a smirk. *Fuck.*

"You feel ready to me." He lifts himself up on his knees, reaching down and aiming my cock up—straight at his ass. He sits back down, my cock sliding between his warm cheeks, and into his even warmer hole. "Mmmmm, yeah..." he groans as I breach him.

My cock flexes involuntarily against the tight heat surrounding it. It feels amazing, though it's hard to fight against the urge to start thrusting up. Rurig's eyes are closed, savoring the feeling of being filled, something I am all too familiar with. He's already taken me to the hilt, and I didn't see an *ounce* of pain on his face while he did it. Nothing but pleasure. With how fast he prepped himself and how fast he's going, he's gotta be an old pro at this. Being married to a couple of other men probably helps. I could learn a thing or two from him. Not sure how—or what—I'd ask, though.

With one hand on my chest to steady himself, Rurig lifts himself off an inch or two before sliding back down. His other hand is still gripping his dick, slowly stroking himself, revealing his wet head each time his foreskin is pulled back. I'm actually kind of jealous, normally when I get fucked my dick is only half-hard at best. I guess I just become so focused on the one thing that my dick just says "meh" to everything else.

I'm biting my lip as the wet heat of his ass slides up and down my length, occasionally snapping my hips up to meet him halfway. This is so much better than jerking off. Rurig's riding picks up speed, but the hand on his cock keeps steady. I reach one hand up to rub across his chest and stomach, watching the way his belly ripples with the movement of his wrist. The skin is soft under my fingers, lined with the occasional stretch mark. I'm not sure if I have a "type," but as far as bodies go, I have yet to find one I didn't like.

With my other hand I grab his balls, thick and weighty against my stomach. He moans when I roll them in my palm, thrusting down onto me hard when I give them a light squeeze. The more I play with them, the faster his hand moves, and more importantly for me, so do his hips. Rurig is all but fucking himself on my cock as he works himself closer to the edge.

"Fuck," he grits out. "If you keep that up, pup, you are going to make me—"

He cuts himself off with a growl, his whole body tensing, including his ass. I squeeze his thighs as he squeezes me, and when he finally unclenches, a thick, hot, rope of cum shoots from the head of his cock, covering me from stomach to neck. He paints the rest of my torso with shots two through six, releasing his cock with a happy sigh when he's finally finished.

While he catches his breath, my cock twitches, still inside of him. He opens one eye, peeking down at me with a soft grin. His body is more relaxed, his belly pressing his softening cock against me. Not sure what comes over me, but I run a finger through the mess he left on my chest, bringing it up to my mouth to taste. That makes him grin even wider.

"I knew I liked you." He bends over, reaching behind my head to pull me up and meet him halfway for a kiss. His tongue slides into my mouth for only a moment before he pulls away, letting me fall back to the bed. "Your turn."

With both his hands on the side of my chest, he starts to ride me again. He resumes the pace he had set for himself earlier, not showing any signs of feeling overstimulated. My hands hold onto his thighs, my own hips snapping up steadily to meet his. He wants me to cum, and I am more than happy to oblige.

Fuck, this feels so good, so different from what I'm used to. I may have to talk to Khazak about doing some more of this. He's got a pretty nice ass himself... A sudden feeling of wrongness pops into my head, thinking about the son of the guy I'm currently inside of, but I shake it off easily. Or maybe it just doesn't feel as wrong as I think, seeing as it's the thing about to push me over the edge.

"Gonna cum," I blurt out, hands tight on Rurig's thighs.

"Good," is his reply, riding me even faster.

I can't help but thrust up when I finally unload, trying to bury myself as deep as possible with each shot. Rurig lets all of his weight fall, leaving me just enough leverage to keep thrusting shallowly. When he's finally drained me and I've stopped moving, he bends over and kisses me again, this one slow, all tongue. He sits up straight with a sigh, looking like a hunter pleased with his catch.

"Spirits, I love that feeling." He grinds himself down, my cock slowly softening inside of him. "But I doubt I need to tell you that."

"Yeah, I'm pretty familiar." It *is* a nice feeling...

"Alright, I suppose it is time to check on—"

"Seriously, Rurig?" Both our heads whip around to look in the open doorway, where somehow we both (okay, so maybe I'm the only one facing this way, whatever) missed a large green man now standing in it: Orlun, Jarek and Rurig's third husband. And he doesn't look too happy. *Uh oh.*

Chapter 3

"What the hell is going on here?" I see Orlun standing in the doorway behind his husband. His husband who is still sitting on my now-deflated cock. I'm frozen, unsure of what to do or say. *Oh gods, how is this happening again?*

"I am pretty sure you know exactly what is going on here, dear," Rurig answers over his shoulder, looking at his husband with a hint of amusement. "Or did Murza work you so hard today that you forgot?"

"You know what I mean." Orlun crosses his arms. "I thought we agreed we would until after I got home tonight before starting with the festivities."

"Do not look at me." Rurig finally moves from his position straddling me, my cock slipping from his hole as he slides off the bed. "Jarek grabbed him first. I am only playing catch up."

"Ah yes, if he did it, why not you as well?" Orlun rolls his eyes. "Very mature."

"If you wanted mature, you would not have married me," Rurig tells him with a grin as he saunters over, kissing the taller man deeply. "I need to check on dinner. Try not to break him!"

Orlun shakes his head with a sigh as he watches his chubby husband exit the room. Then he turns his gaze on me, still naked on my back, evidence of what I just got done doing with said husband all over and around me. I feel like a trapped animal, waiting to be pounced on.

"Is that how my son taught you to greet someone, boy?" He cocks an eyebrow as he looks down at me.

"I, uh, I'm sorry. I don't—"

"Get over here and help me undress." He snaps his fingers and points down at his shoes. "Help me take these boots off."

I stare at him wide eyed before sitting up. "Yes, sir."

I quickly scramble off the bed, something about the older man driving me to obey. Maybe it's his gruff demeanor, maybe it's because he's Khazak's father and I want to please him, hell, maybe it's because he looks a *lot* like Khazak himself, but I kneel down next to his feet, hands already reaching for his laces. An appreciative hum from above me at least tells me I'm doing well.

"That is more like it." I look up to see Orlun unbuttoning his shirt as he watches me work on his boots. "Have you not done this for my son?"

"Uh, no sir." I shake my head. Khazak and I spend most of the day together, so we generally get dressed and undressed at the same time.

"Hmm." He considers me as I help him out of his boots. "For someone who claims to have wanted an avakesh for so long, he certainly does not seem to be training you very well. Then again, he always did like to pamper his pets. That more your style, boy?"

"I don't need pampering." I look up defiantly. What, does he just think I lay around all day?

"Not to worry." He finishes pulling off his shirt. "We have all night to get you trained up properly. Assuming you can take it."

I narrow my eyes at the challenge. "I can take it."

"Good. Come with me." I stand, following someone into the bathroom for the second time today. Orlun stands in front of the mirror, hands already undoing the buttons on his pants. "Turn on the shower."

"Yes, sir." I move to do as asked. Something about the man's callous attitude has me torn between wanting to please him and wanting to prove his assumptions about me wrong

"My son seems quite enamored with you, but I am not sure I like the idea of him sharing a bed with someone who barely a month ago was trying to kill him." I work the knobs of the shower as he talks, the setup largely identical to Khazak's.

"I wasn't actually trying to kill him." I test the water temperature with one hand. "We were both given bad information. It was really just a misunderstanding. Sir."

"So you claim." He finishes stripping, standing in all his naked glory. "I will come to my own conclusions."

"Shower's ready, sir." I step back and try not to stare as he moves past me.

Orlun hums in approval after testing it himself, stepping the rest of the way inside. He stands under the spray, the water cascading down his rippled muscles, and my attempt not to stare goes out the window. He's got a nice body. He's maybe a little less muscular than Khazak, probably because he's retired from active duty, but he's also leaner. Same forest of body hair too, though like his beard, it's more of a salt and pepper color. A throat being cleared draws my eyes up to his face, where a cocked eyebrow is waiting for me. *Guess he wants me to get in with him? At least I'm already... oh god, I've been naked since he walked in the room.* Determined to not look embarrassed, I step inside the shower stall.

"Soap and sponge are behind you." Orlun steps away from the showerhead to make room for me.

I spot them on a shelf easy enough, my body getting wet as I reach for them. When I turn around, Orlun's stance tells me I didn't grab these for myself. No problem. I have some experience in washing tall, muscular orcs. I lather up the sponge, keeping my face neutral as I bring it to his chest. This close, without his clothes on, I can smell all the musk and sweat he worked up during the day. It's...familiar. Pleasant, even.

I scrub the sponge along his skin, holding onto his arm with my free hand to keep myself steady. He has the same tattoo as Khazak on his right pec, a solid black sword with a jagged blade; a visual representation of their last name, Ironstorm. I move to his shoulders and upper arms, eliciting a small groan of approval when I press against his muscles, likely sore from all the lifting. That gives me an idea.

I start to work with a firmer hand, trying to massage him as I wash. I get no complaints, only more groans, so I continue. This is pretty different from my showers with Khazak. Those are a lot more reciprocal with Khazak even taking the lead most of the time. Though to be fair, I'm still pretty new to this whole "sex with men" thing, even if I have done it twice today already. *Does this make two and a half?* My dick seems to think so, already waking up again after getting knocked out by its earlier turn in Rurig's ass. There's something about the way I'm doing this for Orlun—serving him—that is turning me on.

When I'm done with his chest and arms, I move to his stomach, then drop to one knee when it's time to go lower. This puts me face to face with his cock... which looks a lot like Khazak's cock. *Wait, is that a weird thing to think?* I shake the thoughts from my head, focusing on lathering up the man's thick thighs and groin. When it comes time to take care of his package, I avoid any teasing or stroking, trying my best to keep things methodical. I see the appendage twitch a few times, and while I'm pretty sure it's plumped up a little, he hasn't actually indicated he wants more from me. Yet. Like I said before, for some reason, I want to please this man.

When I finish with his lower legs, I feel him moving above me, and I look up to see him stretching his arms above his head, looking back down at me with a satisfied smirk. Then he turns around, leaning his arms against the shower wall to hold himself steady while presenting his back for me. *Time for his other side.*

I stand, re-soaping the sponge to finish the job. I start with his neck and shoulders, changing up my tactics a little. With him facing away from me, I'm a little less nervous about slipping and falling onto him, so while my left hand scrubs with the sponge, the right squeezes and massages the soapy muscles. I hear more groans as I move down to his broad and rippled back. I watch the soap slide down the lines, and it's hard not to trace my fingers over them.

After his back comes his ass, and I'm back to feeling a little nervous. It's hard to wash and massage someone's butt without it seeming sexual. *Maybe that's what he wants?* Either way, kneeling here staring at it isn't gonna wash it any faster, so I soap his cheeks up and get to work. They're thick, green, and covered in the same layer of salt-and-pepper body hair as the rest of him. It's a nice ass on a nice body.

After his butt comes the backs of his thighs and legs, and after *that*, I'm done. Mission complete! I stand while Orlun turns around, still wearing that same satisfied smirk. Placing one hand on my chest, he pushes me back, stepping forward to stand under the shower's spray and rinse off. He continues moving forward, pressing me against the wet stone wall and allowing the water to tumble down his back and shoulders next. He holds me against the wall, his face is only inches from mine, searching for...something.

"Good job, boy," he tells me when he finally steps back. "But you are not done yet."

He leans back, his eyes moving downward. Right to his slowly-filling cock, which my eyes of course lock right onto. Small rivulets of water drip down the shaft, the exposed head poking out from behind his foreskin. He's barely even half hard (*I think*) and I can already tell he's thick. Nothing I can't handle (*I also think*), but still.

"On your knees." Orlun points to the shower floor in front of him, leaving no confusion about what I will be doing next.

"Yes, sir." I sink to my knees once more, sponge and soap behind me, forgotten. Biting my lip, I tentatively reach out a hand toward his cock when a hand tugs on my hair lightly and I look up.

"No hands." Seeing no room for argument on Orlun's face, I can only nod, crossing my arms behind my back.

Still gripping my hair, Orlun pushes his hips forward, guiding himself toward my mouth with his free hand. I open on instinct as he approaches, wet head sliding past my lips with little resistance. This close to his crotch I can smell the soap I used—something lightly floral—and under that just the smallest hint of spiciness, his natural scent already returning. I can't help the small moans that escape as he pushes more of his cock inside me.

Hand still in my hair, he holds me still, unmoving himself other than the occasional pulse of his cock. He savors the feeling of my mouth, making small half-humps, rubbing himself against my tongue. With a growl, he pulls back before plunging himself forward, burying even more of his cock in my mouth and breaching my throat.

"Not bad," comes the voice from above as its owner plunders my mouth.

Unable to respond or look up with a gullet full of dick, I close my eyes and focus on relaxing my throat. Orlun is doing most of the work as he fucks my face, though the hand in my hair is pushing and pulling, almost like he's trying to get me to meet him halfway. He's not going deep enough to make me gag, at least not yet. I'm still holding my arms behind me, sitting up and balancing on my knees as the shower's spray hits my shoulders, water sliding down my back.

The combination of the water against my back, the heat of the shower stall, and the rhythmic way he slides in and out of my mouth makes it easy to zone out. I can feel drool escaping out of the sides of my mouth, but if there were ever a place to not care about that, it would be a shower. And I *really* don't care right now. So much so that I don't even notice the second hand moving to the back of my head.

Can't say the same for the rest of the cock being pushed into my throat, though. Definitely notice that.

My eyes go wide as my air is cut off more than I'm expecting, meaning completely. I flail my arms out ready to either push him away or catch myself, but there's no need. Only a moment later, my head is released, allowing me to pull off completely. I sit back on my legs, catching my breath as the water rinses my face.

"Good boy." Orlun smiles—an actual smile—as he runs a hand over his dick. "Turn the shower off, then grab a towel from the rack."

It's a simple enough order to follow, and once I'm done rinsing off all the drool, I stand and turn off the water. I do my best not to drip all over the floor as I reach for the towel just outside the shower. Once it is in my hands, Orlun stands in front of me, waiting for me to finish what I started.

Drying someone off is thankfully much easier than washing them, and after running the towel over his head (drying off someone's hair is weird), I move on to his chest and shoulders, working my way down his body until he turns for me and I work my way back up. When I'm finished, he takes the towel from me, touching up any spots I missed before tossing it back at my chest.

"You can use that to dry yourself as well," he tells me as he exits the shower.

"...Gee, thanks sir." I wince at my tone as soon as the words leave my mouth. *Really not doing yourself any favors, David.*

"I am sure my son has fun spanking that attitude out of you." Orlun chuckles ahead of me.

"He certainly tries to, sir." I quickly dry myself and return the towel to the rack as Orlun leaves the bathroom.

Some of my nerves return as I enter the bedroom. Don't have to be a genius to know what's coming next. Orlun is standing by the nightstand, already pulling the oil from the drawer. He looks over to me in the doorway.

"All fours." He points to the bed.

I clamber onto the bed on my hands and knees, waiting for Orlun to join me. I jump a little when I feel the mattress dip, then overcorrect by staying stock still right after. Why the hell am I so nervous? I've done this twice today already, one of which he walked in on.

"Nothing to be scared of, boy," Orlun tries to calm me as he kneels at my side, hand running from my back to my butt. "I know what I am doing."

Hard to argue that with a man who has two husbands, two husbands I have already had sex with today. He moves behind me, hands rubbing along my body, squeezing my ass gently before giving it a few smacks. Grabbing it with both hands, he pries me apart, making me blush as he inspects me closely. One of the hands releases me, only for its fingers to slide across my hole a second later, making me shiver.

"At least Jarek already opened you up for me." He teases me before gently slipping a finger inside. "Still slick too."

Next I hear the familiar *schlick* sounds of a slick hand being run over someone's shaft. I tense when he moves into position, his knees brushing the insides of my legs as he has me spread them even wider. He slides himself up and down my crack, slowly rubbing the head across my hole.

"Easy does it, boy," Orlun tries to calm my nerves as he takes aim at his target. "This is nothing you cannot handle."

Easy for you to say. The older orc begins to breach me, one hand on my hips as my hole is entered for the second time today. He's definitely the biggest of the three men in the house, but I don't think he's any larger than Khazak. I'm just having a hard time relaxing. Not that it's stopping Orlun from making sure I'm filled to the absolute brim.

"*Spirits* you are tight," Orlun hisses, squeezing my ass with his hands again. "Even if you were not attractive, I could certainly see *this* being enough of a reason for him to keep you."

Thanks, I think? I don't say it out loud. I don't think he'd like that.

"That said, you have been performing admirably so far, boy." He punctuates his sentence with a spank. "Perhaps my son has not been so lax in training you after all."

He isn't looking for an answer, so I don't give one. Not sure I really could anyway once he really starts fucking me. He pulls out almost entirely on the first stroke, pushing back in at the same speed, and he's soon fucking me with the confidence of an old pro. Which again, two husbands, so...

That seems to be his fuck-MO, pulling back enough to leave just his head in so he can spear me with the full length of his cock on every in-stroke. Having apparently enjoyed giving my ass a few smacks earlier, he starts to spank me in time with his thrusts, switching sides each time and turning my cheeks a nice shade of pink.

All of this adds up to me feeling amazing. Sparks of pleasure shoot up my spine as my prostate is teased, mixed with the small bursts of pain from the spanking. I can feel the familiar tension of an anal orgasm starting to build in the background. *Gods, am I really this easy?* As the orgasm starts to crest and my toes curl, I'd have to say the answer is yes. I moan into the mattress, riding the wave of pleasure that I know is going to return sooner rather than later.

"And now, my turn." I can hear the hunger in Orlun's voice as his fucking slows to a stop.

One of his hands reaches down and grabs the front of my right thigh while the other pushes down on my back, encouraging me to lay flat. He moves with me as I go, slotting his body over mine and taking my wrists in his hands, all without his cock ever leaving my ass. With a growl, he circles his hips, grinding into me.

Satisfied with our new position, Orlun puts both of his feet on the inside of my legs, spreading me even further as he draws his hips up. He no longer seems concerned with long-dicking me, making it only a few inches before fucking me into the mattress. He sets a fast pace, the bed creaking with the force of his thrusts. It doesn't take long before I can feel myself cumming again, crying out weakly as I'm fucked through it.

"Well now you are just," Orlun grunts after a particularly strong thrust, "being selfish."

After another minute or two of bouncing on my ass, there's a stutter in the thrusts of the orc on top of me. With a muffled roar, he slams himself down, cock pulsing as he starts to cum. The hands around my wrists squeeze tight as he breeds me, adding his load to the one Jarek left in me earlier. After a few more short, abortive thrusts, he finally collapses, sweaty chest meeting sweaty back.

We lay there, catching our breaths as we recover. Or at least I do my best to with the huge orc on top of me. Aware of his weight pinning me down, he rolls us onto our sides, cock slipping from my hole as we move. I whimper at its loss, and I can hear Orlun chuckle as he strokes a hand down my chest.

"You did very well, boy," the gravelly voice speaks low into my ear, making me shudder. "You have my approval."

Won't lie—that sentence makes me feel all nice and warm inside. I snuggle back against the orc who just got done using me in more ways than one. *It's the least he can do.* He doesn't object, content to hold me there on the bed while I rest. I relax so much I don't even hear when Rurig steps into the room.

"Aww, that makes a cute picture." I can't help but twitch a little in surprise at his sudden appearance. "If you boys are all finished, go get cleaned up; dinner is ready."

"Yes, dear," Orlun says with a laugh, ruffling my hair and kissing the back of my head before untangling us and standing.

"So, are you satisfied?" Rurig asks his husband as he walks to the bathroom.

"For now," he answers from inside. "We will see what happens after dinner."

These men are going to kill me.

Chapter 4

I follow Orlun into the bathroom on shaky legs. I spot him at the far end of the counter, washing his dick in the sink. He smirks at me as I pass him, going for the toilet because I swear it feels like I've got a gallon of orc cum in me. He ruffles my hair when he's finished, while I'm still sitting down feeling it leak out of me, and then I'm alone.

After I finish cleaning up, I return to the bedroom, looking for my clothes but only spotting my jockstrap and pants. Taking this as a subtle order, I redress my lower half before venturing out. Rurig said dinner was ready, so I aim for the dining room, where I find all three orcs seated and waiting for me. Rurig and Orlun are on one side of the table while Jarek is on the other with an empty seat next to him. Everyone is shirtless, so at least I don't need to feel weird about that.

"There you are," Rurig notes my entrance. "Was worried we might have worn you out."

"It'll take more than that, sirs," I say perhaps a little too cockily as I take my seat.

"We will see about that," Orlun replies.

Rurig says a quick blessing and we all dig in. The stew I helped him with is delicious, the meat juicy and tender. All around me are the sounds of slurping and chewing, as well as the occasional mumbled "thank you" to Rurig and me for cooking. It's a few minutes before people have had enough to slow down a little and talk.

"How were Murza and Yanik?" Rurig asks after wiping his mouth.

"They are doing well," Orlun replies. "Tasha will be finishing school in just a few months."

"Will she be moving out?" Jarek asks next.

"Not just yet." Orlun shakes his head." I think she has enjoyed having her mothers' attention all to herself."

"Do you think Urza or Ignatz will feel that way one day?" Jarek almost sounds a little sad when he asks.

"Spirits, I hope not," Rurig says with a sigh. "It took Yogik over two years to leave."

"You were *just* complaining a few days ago about how none of your children ever come home to visit and that you wished none of them had ever left," Jarek reveals from his seat.

"Quiet you." Rurig points at his husband with his spoon, giving him a very un-serious glare. "Do any of your siblings still live at home, David?"

"Only my sister. She just turned sixteen." *And is probably pretty pissed off that I missed her birthday.*

"I for one cannot wait until we have the house back to ourselves," Orlun adds. "Finally get back the freedom to do what we want around here."

"Yeah, we know all about the kind of things you want to do around here, *usan*." Jarek looks at me and wiggles his eyebrows and I chuckle. I get the feeling that we have the same sense of humor, though I bet he gets spanked a *lot* less, if at all.

"Is that so, *tuto*?" Orlun smirks at his husband's challenge, using an equally cute-sounding nickname. "Perhaps after dinner I will test that."

After dinner is finished, we bring our dishes into the kitchen where Orlun and Jarek take care of the bulk of the cleanup. While they are doing that, Rurig brings me into the den where he pulls out a deck of cards to teach me the rules of a game called *uk'pad'uk*. It takes me a minute—mostly because I have problems reading the cards—but I get the hang of it by the time Orlun and Jarek rejoin us.

The game actually reminds me a lot of Spades, with everyone playing a single card each hand. I just run into issues when it comes to remembering which cards beat which other cards or what certain combinations mean. This ends up leading to a lot of laughs when I screw something up or groans when I inadvertently play something that wins the hand. It's not happening on purpose, but a side-effect of me not really knowing what I'm doing means I've got a *great* poker face.

"You are *killing* me, boy," Orlun groans when I take yet another hand and win the game. He turns to Rurig on his left. "It was a mistake to let you teach him to play."

"Do not blame me because your skills are getting rusty with age, dear husband," Rurig snarks, but then leans over to kiss his husband on the cheek.

Jarek gathers up the cards and straightens the stack. "So, do we want to play another round, or..." He looks between both his spouses as he trails off—but not me.

"I think that is enough for the time being." Orlun stands, and then so does the rest of the group.

"What are we doing now?" I ask the obvious question.

"*You* are going to go back to your bedroom to remove those pants." Orlun points to me before turning his finger on himself. "Then you are going to come find us in *our* bedroom."

"I... Yes, sir." I nod, mentally shaking my head for not connecting the dots sooner.

The four of us split up, me down one hallway and the three of them down another. When I return to Khazak's bedroom, I find the rest of my clothes folded over the back of his desk chair, explaining their earlier disappearance. It doesn't take me more than a half a minute to get my pants off, which doesn't feel weird itself, but walking through their house with my ass hanging out definitely does.

I enter the bedroom to find all three men sitting on the large bed, all naked, all of their cocks raised to at least half-mast. Orlun is sitting in the center with Jarek on his right, the two in a deep lip-lock. On his left is Rurig, who is leaning over to take one of Orlun's nipples into his mouth. Both of Orlun's arms are thrown over his husbands' shoulders, and when he notices me enter, he lightly tugs them both away, all three settling back against the headboard.

"Come here, boy." The orc-in-charge crooks his finger at me, before pointing at his crotch. "You can start with me."

"Yes, sir." I nod, subconsciously licking my lips.

I climb onto the bed, crawling to lay stomach-down between his spread thighs. His cock, which I am already intimately acquainted with (along with every other dick in the room), hangs heavy over his ball sack, twitching as it slowly finishes coming to life. Reaching to grasp it with one hand, I push myself up on my elbows to bring my mouth level with the appendage, pulling back the foreskin and licking over the head before attempting to swallow down more.

A hand tightens on my head, but it's not Orlun's. From the angle, I think it's Rurig. He pushes me down farther onto Orlun's cock, holding me in place for a few seconds before allowing me to come up for air. Then he pushes me to sink back down and remains on my head as I bob up and down on the hard length.

Above me, I can hear the sound of lips smacking against each other as two of the men resume kissing. With my right hand wrapped around Orlun to hold him steady, Jarek grabs my free left hand and pulls it toward his crotch, wrapping my fingers around his dick. Taking the hint, I do my best to jerk and squeeze his cock to his liking, but it's a bit difficult with my attention focused elsewhere.

Orlun's cock has grown to its full size, thick and heavy with my lips stretched wide around it. The hand on my head has not let up, and I don't think it will be much longer before my mouth starts to go numb. The musk coming from Orlun's crotch is heady, a combination of our sex from earlier and what he's worked up now. It helps me to zone out and push myself a little further than I normally would.

"Alright, enough of that." The hand on my head tugs me off and I look up at Orlun. "I cannot keep you all to myself."

The hand never quite leaves my hair, and I'm shuffled over to my right to lay between a different set of legs—Rurig's. As I am brought face to face with his crotch, there is some shuffling on the bed to my left.

Before I can see what's happening, I'm being drawn forward so Rurig can slot himself between my lips.

I didn't get a chance to suck Rurig earlier. It seemed like he knew exactly what he wanted, and I wasn't going to argue with him. Especially not since it meant getting my own dick sucked and sat on. Now, its thickness stretches my lips, almost enough to make it difficult to go farther down. But I'm nothing if not a trooper.

My free hand is grabbed and pulled over once again, and from the feel of the dick in my hand, I'd guess that Jarek slid over into Orlun's spot. So where did the other orc go? When I feel the weight on the bed shifting behind me, I figure it out, and when I feel the hands on my ass, I realize why he's back there.

Without a word, the hands on my ass spread my cheeks, and I feel the flats of his tusks pushing against them a second before I feel his tongue hit my hole. I moan around the meat in my mouth as Orlun lathes my ass with his tongue. His hands squeeze my cheeks, before one of them rears back and smacks me, making my jump and gasp. The deeper his tongue probes, the rougher his hands seem to get, kneading them like fleshy dough in between spanks. Between the hands behind me, the one on my head, and the dick in my mouth, I'm having a hard time focusing.

"He has a thing for tasting himself after fucking someone," Jarek informs me from above.

"Pretty sure I can taste you, too," Orlun adds, tearing away from my ass for a second before jumping back in.

Rurig laughs, sending more of his cock into my mouth. "He does this to one of us almost every night."

I don't doubt it. The things Orlun's tongue is doing to me are driving me crazy; the man has some skills. I can hear him behind me as he hungrily eats my hole, all growls and slurps. He's all but fucking me with his tongue, sliding in and out past my ring, making me twitch and whimper all over his husband's cock.

"Are you both planning to hog his holes the rest of the night, or will I be allowed to get in there at some point?" Jarek complains from my left.

"I do not know what you are whining about. You were the one who jumped on him before either of us even had the chance," Rurig replies dryly.

"It is called *taking initiative.*" I can hear the cocky grin on Jarek's face. "And clearly I am going to have to do the same thing here."

My hand is removed from Jarek's cock, and I feel more movement on my left. It doesn't feel like he's moved away, and when I notice the light being blocked, I turn my head to see from the corner of my eye that he is kneeling against Rurig's thigh. Rather than replacing his cock in my hand, I feel it tapping against my shoulder.

"Always so impatient, *tuto,*" Rurig jokes, pulling me off his cock.

I already know what's coming, and my head is lifted and turned to the left to accept Jarek's rock-hard and leaking dick. He is thankfully less thick than his husbands, so my mouth no longer feels like it's being stretched to its limit. Jarek also seems happy to do most of the work for me, thrusting forward into my face. After a minute of that, he releases me and pushes me back toward Rurig's cock. The two of them continue to swap my mouth back and forth like that, all while Orlun remains behind me, face buried in my butt.

"Delicious," Orlun praises me (or at least my hole) with another spank. "But I think it is time to fill you with something else."

Orlun leaves his spot behind me, as does Jarek at my side. I crawl backward from between Rurig's legs, only to be flipped onto my back on the center of the bed next to him. My own cock, which has been completely hard since Orlun pulled me onto his dick, smacks against my belly. As Rurig and Jarek both kneel by my head, I catch them looking at it appreciatively.

"Mmmm," Rurig hums as he snakes a hand down my chest and stomach to reach for it. Taking it in hand, he squeezes me before stroking me slowly, just teasing. "You get a chance to ride this thing?" Rurig asks Jarek.

"Not yet." Jarek shakes his head, looking at my length with consideration. It twitches in response, never considering that possibility before now.

"You can both use him and his cock for whatever you would like," Orlun tells the both of them as he rejoins us on the bed, kneeling between my legs. "*After* I am through with him."

"*Yes, sir,*" Jarek says mockingly, and I see the hint of a smile cross Orlun's face.

Orlun lifts and spreads my legs as he moves closer, pushing them back to look at my hole. Rurig and Jarek's cocks are both at eye level, but neither of them moves, more interested in watching what Orlun is doing for the time being. The man uncorks the bottle of oil he must have retrieved when he first left the bed, and I watch mesmerized as he pours some into his hand and strokes it over the length of his prick. Then, with the same oil-covered hand, he reaches toward my ass, smearing the remaining slick across my hole.

I am still wet and open from not just the very thorough rimming he just got done giving me, but also the *two* fuckings I received earlier today. He pushes in a single finger, not stopping until my hole has swallowed all of it. He pumps it in and out only once before adding a second, using both to check that I am still stretched enough. Satisfied, he removes them, shuffling even closer while still pressing my legs toward my chest. Releasing one to aim himself, he lays the head of his cock against my rim and pushes inside.

"Good," he says with a groan as he bottoms out. "Still nice and tight," he continues, as if he was auditioning me.

"Still huge and thick," I say with a groan of my own. I know I've already taken this once today, but holy shit.

Orlun chuckles at my comment, giving me some time to adjust before he starts moving. Jarek and Rurig begin tapping themselves against my face, each trying to convince me to use their dick like some sort of sexual pacifier. Supposing it's better than nothing, I start with Rurig, taking the first few inches into my mouth and nursing on him before turning my head to do the same to Jarek. Above me, I watch as the two lean over me to kiss, at least until Rurig's belly blocks my view. As the sounds of their kissing fills the room, Orlun begins to slide back, taking some of his cock with him before pushing back in.

The four of us fall into a rhythm so quickly that I can't help but wonder if the three husbands haven't done this before with some other unsuspecting boy. Orlun certainly seems to know what he's doing, fucking me just as well as he did only hours ago. Each pass of his prick over my prostate has me squirming, the thick member stretching my walls to their limit.

Clearly the man only needed the one time to become an expert in using my hole. It only takes him a few more strokes to make me cum dry, Rurig's dick muffling my moans.

"Alright, my young, impatient husband," Orlun says to Jarek, pausing after fucking me through my orgasm. "Your turn."

He doesn't need to be told twice, breaking away from Rurig and leaving his position by my face to replace Orlun between my legs. Orlun does the same, taking up position near my head and leaning in to kiss Rurig. His cock, which has just been in my ass, presses against my cheek, waiting for its turn. Between my legs, I hear what sounds like Jarek spitting before my legs are being lifted and I am once again filled. *Fuck.*

Jarek doesn't have quite the same skill as his older and more experienced husband, nor is his dick as big, but he's no slouch. He still knows what he's doing, fucking me good enough to make my toes curl. I turn my head toward Orlun, tasting for the first time a cock that's been pulled from my hole. All I can taste is musk, and cum, and under all of it the familiar and distinct flavor of *cock*. As Orlun drives himself into my gullet, I feel myself cresting over the edge again, the anal orgasm rolling through my body.

"Okay, your turn again, *usan*." I almost miss the pet name when I feel Jarek pulling out.

This time rather than switch places, both top men seem content to remain below my waist, leaving Rurig my upper body to play with on his own. He pushes back into my mouth at the same time Orlun re-enters my ass, but from the brief look at his face that I get, I can tell he's already thinking of something else.

"Time to see how good this boy is at eating ass." That's all the warning I get before I see the massive tree trunk that is Rurig's thigh pass over my head as he moves to straddle my head. I take a deep breath as the large green ass is lowered toward my face.

Another first, probably shouldn't be the first thing that goes through my mind, but it is. The second is that my tongue should be out if I'm going to do this properly. The orc thankfully isn't actually resting all of his weight on me, and the only things I can smell are sweat and musk, so I dare to dart out to lick along his hole, enjoying the shudder I feel above me in response. As I get more comfortable with rimming, Rurig relaxes and presses me farther into the mattress.

"Careful. If we smother him, Khazak will never let us hear the end of it," Orlun jokingly warns as he fucks me.

"If he dies, he dies," Rurig jokes (I hope) as he grinds his ass against my face.

Orlun and Jarek both continue to fuck me, swapping off every few minutes. Thanks to Rurig blocking my view, the only way I have of telling who is currently occupying my nether regions is by the size of the dick rearranging them. Rurig keeps sitting on my face, lifting up now and again to ensure I'm still able to breathe. From the way I can feel his balls slapping against my chest, I think he's jerking off. I'm doing alright, though I do think the lack of oxygen is making me feel a little loopy, but not necessarily in a bad way.

"*Shit,* open wide." Rurig suddenly lifts off my face completely, quickly shoving his cock in my mouth as it explodes. I swallow as fast as I can, his load thankfully not as large as the one from this afternoon.

"I am right behind you," Jarek, who I can now see is fucking me, grits out.

I can feel the speed of his thrusts pick up, his grip on my legs tightening as he chases his orgasm. He finally cums with a low groan, slamming his hips against mine and holding my legs tightly to his chest. I watch the droplets of sweat drip down to his belly, his dick pulsing within me as it unloads for the second time today. When he's done, he watches as he slips from my body, clearly enjoying the sight of my used hole before handing me off to Orlun.

Who is looking down at me with a *very* determined look on his face.

Uh oh.

After all of the day's activity, his cock slides into me with ease, not stopping until I've taken it to the hilt. I think I can feel him somewhere just below my lungs. After giving me a few test strokes, he begins pounding away with abandon, my sloppy hole no match for the thick battering ram of his cock. Combined with everything Jarek just got finished doing, I'm close, just needing that last little push which ends up coming in the form of Orlun reaching up, grabbing me by the neck, and *squeezing.*

Oh my gods, this is so fucking hot.

I cum with a high-pitched whine, my hands scrabbling for purchase against the mattress as my ass pulses and fights against the thick member forcing it open. The feeling of my hole spasming around him is all Orlun needs, and with a *roar*, he crashes our bodies together, crushing his lips against my own. His hips thrust with every shot of cum that leaves his cock, each one pressing us closer together.

We are both breathing heavily when Orlun finally lifts off of me, lowering my legs to the mattress but not pulling himself from my ass. His face is pleased, *sated* even, and a quick glance to my left reveals Rurig and Jarek cuddling at our side. I can't help but smile at the scene. I'm not sure I'm going to survive the next few days, but at least it'll be a fun way to go out.

"What the hell is going on here?!" All four of our heads spin to see Khazak entering the room. *What?!*

"Son. What are you doing home already?" Orlun sounds like a kid caught with his hand in the cookie jar. Or his cock in...me. *Oh god.* Seemingly realizing the same thing I just did, he moves quickly from between my legs, and I fail to suppress a whimper when he pulls out too fast. Orlun moves to sit with his husbands, leaving me naked and exposed on my back in front of my owner.

My owner who looks angry.

"Two of the other delegations canceled and discussions ended early." Khazak looks between the four of us, the displeasure apparent on his face. "I have been knocking on the door for almost five minutes. So sorry to see that I am interrupting."

"It is not what it looks like," Rurig speaks up, and my head turns. *It's not?!*

"Oh, then please tell me what you all are doing in bed with my avakesh!" He sounds angry.

No one says anything, so I find myself speaking up first. "I thought... They told me this was a tradition?"

"It is an *old* tradition." He looks accusatorily between all three of his fathers. "One that fell out of common practice *years* ago."

My eyes go wide at his revelation. "I-I didn't know, I swear! I had no idea! I only went along with—"

Khazak holds his hand up to silence me. "Obviously, there is only one thing to be done about this."

"What's that?" I look up at him nervously.

"I am just going to have to restake my claim." As he speaks, he begins pulling off his clothing, climbing onto the bed once he's naked. Taking hold of my ankle, he yanks my body toward him, lifting and holding my legs the same as his father just finished doing to me. With a evil glint in his eyes, he—

♥

"Ny, you alright?" Ragnar's voice makes me jump in my seat, almost shrieking in surprise.

"I'm fine!" I quickly slam shut the journal I've been writing in.

My answer has him eyeing me suspiciously, no doubt taking in my flushed face and heavy breathing. There's also the matter of the erection currently tenting my pants, but even without that, he's always been a good detective. Look, I can't help it if I get turned on by my own writing. I'm just that good!

"What are you—" He stops mid-sentence when his gaze lands on the journal. "Are you writing your weird 'erotic friend fiction' again?"

"It's not weird!" I defend, immediately giving myself away. *Dammit.* "Our friend T'nah does it too."

"*Your* friend T'nah. And I've also told you that *she's* weird." He shakes his head. "I would always catch her staring at my ass in school."

"Can you blame her? It's a pretty nice ass." I give my Sir my best cheesy grin, one I stole from David before he left the city.

"Oh yeah?" he starts, looking over his shoulder as he walks away from me. "Well, do you want to follow me to the bedroom and do something with this nice ass before it goes in for its shift in an hour?"

"You're gonna let me top?!" I stand excitedly. *He almost never lets me top!*

"I dunno. Not sure I can compete with whatever little fantasies you've been writing down in your book..." He teases, already walking toward the bedroom.

I quickly push in my chair and follow. I can finish my story later. Right now, I need to do some research for my next one.

Property of:

Nylan

About the Author

Dominic N. Ashen is an author and avid reader, with a heavy focus on gay, BDSM-themed erotica. After spending his youth in search of books with characters who were more like himself–queer ones, specifically–he decided to start creating some of his own. His stories star queer protagonists, most often gay and bisexual men, and feature heavy themes of dominance, submission, and all sorts of kink. Dominic loves the fantasy, sci-fi, and horror genres, with a penchant for writing longer stories where he is able to weave in the sex and kink right alongside the plot.

dominicashen.com

facebook.com/dom.n.ashen

instagram.com/dom.n.ashen

twitter.com/DomNAshen

LGBT Erotica

Dominic Ashen
Steel & Thunder
Storms & Sacrifice

Grayson Ace
How I Got Here
First Year Out of
the Closet
You're Only a Top?
You're Only a Bottom?

I Think I'm a
Serial Swiper
Lookin in All the
Wrong Places

Leo Sparx
Before Alexander
Claiming Alexander
Taming Alexander
Saving Alexander

Fantasy, SciFi, & Paranormal Romance

Beau Lake
The Beast Beside Me
The Beast Within Me
Taming the Beast: Novella
The Beast After Me
Charming the Beast: Novella
The Beast Like Me
An Eye for Emeralds
Swimming in Sapphires
Pining for Pearls

D. Lambert
To Walk into the Sands
Rydan
Celebrant
Northlander
Esparan
King
Traitor
His Last Name

Danielle Orsino
Locked Out of Heaven
Thine Eyes of Mercy
From the Ashes
Kingdom Come

J.M. Paquette
Klauden's Ring
Solyn's Body
The Inbetween
Hannah's Heart
Call Me Forth
Invite Me In
Keep Me Close

Lyra R. Saenz
Prelude
Falsetto in the Woods: Novella
Ragtime Swing
Sonata
Song of the Sea
The Devil's Trill

Bercuese
To Heal a Songbird
Ghost March
Nocturne

T.S. SIMONS
Antipodes
The Liminal Space
Ouroboros
Caim
Sessrúmnir

TY CARLSON
The Bench
The Favorite

VALERIE WILLIS
Cedric: The Demonic Knight
Romasanta: Father of
Werewolves
The Oracle: Keeper of the
Gaea's Gate
Artemis: Eye of Gaea
King Incubus: A New Reign

V.C. WILLIS
Prince's Priest
Priest's Assassin

DISCOVER MORE AT
4HorsemenPublications.com

www.ingramcontent.com/pod-product-compliance
Lightning Source LLC
Chambersburg PA
CBHW050428110726
47899CB00008B/2900